Fairy Tales

by Stan Cullimore

Contents

Longman

Baby Bear and the Three Fairies

One day Baby Bear went for a walk.
He went into the woods.

He saw a little house.
"Who lives here?" said Baby Bear.
He went inside.

There was a table inside the house.
It had three bowls of cornflakes on it.

The first bowl was too big.
The second bowl was too small.
The third bowl was just right.

"I shall eat these cornflakes," said Baby Bear.
So he did!
Then he went up the stairs.

There were three beds.
The first bed was too hard.
The second bed was too soft.
The third bed was just right.

"I shall sleep in this bed," said Baby Bear.
So he did!

Three fairies flew in to the house.
"It's good to be home," said Father Fairy.
"It's good to be home," said Mother Fairy.
"Someone has eaten your cornflakes!" said
Baby Fairy.

The three fairies flew up the stairs.
"I'm going to bed," said Father Fairy.
"So am I," said Mother Fairy.
"There is a bear in my bed!" said Baby Fairy.

Baby Bear woke up.
He saw the three fairies.
"Help!" cried Baby Bear.
He ran out of the house and all the way home!

The Flapjack Fairy

Once upon a time an old man made a flapjack.
He put it in the oven to cook.
When he opened the oven ... a Flapjack Fairy
jumped out!

"I'm going to eat you," said the old man.
"You can't eat me," cried the Flapjack Fairy.
"I can fly away!"

The Flapjack Fairy flew out of the window and flew down the road as fast as she could.

A mouse saw the Flapjack Fairy.
"I'm going to eat you," said the mouse.
"You can't eat me," cried the Flapjack Fairy. "I can fly away!"

The Flapjack Fairy flew over the mouse and
flew down the road as fast as she could.
Then she came to a river.
She was tired after all that flying.

"Hello," said a fox.
"You can't eat me," cried the Flapjack Fairy. "I can fly away!"

"You look too tired to fly. Let me help you cross the river," said the fox.
"Thank you," said the Flapjack Fairy.

The Flapjack Fairy jumped on the fox's back. "You would be much safer if you sat on my head," said the fox.

The Flapjack Fairy jumped on the fox's head.

"You would be much safer if you were in my tummy," said the fox.
The fox opened his mouth and the Flapjack Fairy jumped inside.

"Munch, munch, MUNCH!" went the fox.

And that was the end of the Flapjack Fairy.

Little Fly Along Fairy

One day Little Fly Along Fairy was bored.
"Mum," she said. "I'm bored."
Her Mum had an idea. "Why don't you take
this cake and go to see your granny?"
"That's a good idea," said Little Fly Along Fairy.

So she put the cake in her basket and put on her best pair of wings.
Then she opened the front door and went off to see her granny.

"Remember," shouted Mum. "Stay on the path."
"Why?" asked Little Fly Along Fairy.
"Because that nasty wolf lives in the woods,"
said Mum.
"And he eats little fly along fairies!"

Little Fly Along Fairy flew along the path.
"What a lovely day," she said. "I think I shall
pick some flowers for Granny."
She flew away from the path. Suddenly she
stopped.

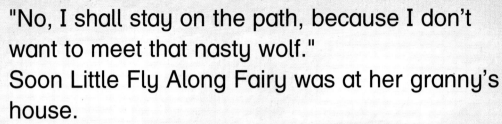

"No, I shall stay on the path, because I don't want to meet that nasty wolf."
Soon Little Fly Along Fairy was at her granny's house.

"Hello," said Little Fly Along Fairy.
"Come in," said a voice from the bedroom.
Little Fly Along Fairy went in to the bedroom.
"Why are you in bed, Granny?" she asked.

"Because I'm not feeling very well," said the voice. "Now come over here."
Little Fly Along Fairy went over and took the cake out of her basket.
"What big, hairy hands you have got, Granny," she said.

"All the better to hold you with," said the voice.
"Now sit down by my side."
Little Fly Along Fairy sat down. "What big,
sharp teeth you have, Granny."
"All the better to eat you with," cried the voice.
Little Fly Along Fairy screamed.

Just then the window blew open and Granny
flew into the room.
"That's not me in bed," she cried. "It's that
nasty wolf."

Granny picked up a broom and chased the wolf
out of the house.
"Go, Granny, go!" shouted Little Fly Along
Fairy.

A few minutes later Granny came back inside
the house.

"Now what shall we do?" asked Little Fly
Along Fairy.

"Eat up all that lovely cake!" replied Granny.
So they did.